Historical reference and inspiration: The Mighty Aztecs, a National Geographic book, based to some extent on word of mouth accounts by indigenous people extoling the splendor of the Toltecs.

To order additional copies of this book, contact:
Xlibris
844-714-8691
www.Xlibris.com
Orders@Xlibris.com

ISBN: Softcover   978-1-9845-8654-4
       Hardcover   978-1-4415-6340-8
       EBook   978-1-9845-8655-1

Library of Congress Control Number: 2008934743

Print information available on the last page.

Rev. date: 08/14/2020

Table of Contents

The Ghost Tree

1 The Contest

More than four-hundred years before Columbus came to America, the great Toltec civilization flourished in Southern Mexico. Their famous Emperor, Quetzalcoatl, meaning, Feathered Serpent, took his name from the all-powerful god of creation. Despising the bloodthirsty religious practices observed by other priest kings, Quetzalcoatl honored his gods with offerings of flowers and butterflies.

The Toltecs, being artists and spinners of the spirit, considered weaving a symbolic art. Tonantzin, the great mother of all life, goddess of destiny and weaver of the threads of fortune, blessed dedicated weavers and their work.

When a proclamation rang forth from Emperor Quetzalcoatl's balcony, the Royal City of Tula buzzed with activity. "Women of

1

our empire!" his herald proclaimed. "Princess Itotia invites all the weavers in her father's kingdom to compete in creating a tapestry designed to bring good fortune to her marriage with Governor Patli of Texcoco! The creator of the winning design shall be proclaimed Royal Weaver. After the wedding, the Royal Standard-bearer shall display the tapestry before the bride and bridegroom as they lead the parade of the Spring Equinox down the glittering Causeway of Jade."

News of the princess's challenge traveled throughout Quetzalcoatl's realm, even to the remote mountain village where Grandmother Atl lived with her orphaned granddaughter, Nemimati.

In the economically and culturally thriving Toltec empire, Grandmother Atl's house was thatched simply with tall blond reeds gathered from the shores of Lake Cuanuac. From her front porch perched high on a cliff, she and her granddaughter could look down on the black spider monkeys playing in the green trees growing on the steep hillside below. The cool breezes at this higher elevation also cleared the flying insects away.

Still, not everything in Grandmother Atl and Nemimati's world was perfect. As she grew older, Grandmother Atl was finding it increasingly difficult to negotiate the steep path to her house. This worried Nemimati.

One day, before beginning the tiring climb to their home, Nemimati looked up at her grandmother with sparkling eyes. "I wish we could move to the city of Tula and live and work in the Royal Palace!" she exclaimed.

"How could we do that, dear?" Grandmother Atl asked.

Nemimati eagerly explained. "You could design the princess' tapestry and accept the position of Royal Weaver!"

Grandmother Atl smiled. "I would love to, child, but I have already asked Goddess Tonantzin to send me an omen for the winning design, and so far, she has remained silent. Also, my eyesight is failing."

"Don't worry," Nemimati replied. "I can see very well. Pray to the goddess again and I will run ahead and get everything ready."

Grandmother Atl raised her eyebrows. "Alright, Nemimati, maybe if you help me, we can win the princess' contest."

2 Nemimati's Adventure

Grandmother Atl knew how to brew vivid dyes from jungle plants and seeds. To make beautiful tints to color her Grandmother's cottons, Nemimati kindled fires in a large adobe firebox and then helped her grandmother put three cauldrons of bark and berries to brew over the flames. When the dyes in the kettles were dark and rich, they set them on a wooden table to cool. Pleased with their work, Grandmother Atl considered her next task.

"Nemimati, why don't you spin thread for me while I go to the village. Perhaps bartering with vendors for tiny beads and fine feathers will inspire me! I have been trying to decide on colors for the tapestry. Also, let's be on the alert for omens from Tonantzin!"

"I will keep on the lookout, Grandmother," Nemimati answered. "Be sure to step carefully as you walk down the path to the village."

"Don't worry, I will go slowly. And make sure you finish your chores," Grandmother Atl replied. She then balanced a big, round, handwoven reed basket containing some of her handicraft on her head, and set out along the steep path that wound down around the hill, to Cuanuac, to visit the vendors.

Anticipating that her grandmother would stay in the village until sunset to gossip with her friends, Nemimati went into the forest to play before sitting down to spin.

While skipping lightly across the pools of water left by the last tropical shower, from behind a patch of ferns, she noticed a glimmer of gold. When she went to investigate, to her surprise, she found a bright little frog with suction toes.

Wondering if Tonantzin had sent this unusual frog as an omen that the tapestry should feature yellow and gold, she took the frog home to show her grandmother when she returned later that evening.

"I shall name you Costi, which means gold," she said, picking him up and nestling him in her woven waist-wrap.

Arriving back at her grandmother's house, Nemimati looked around for a container the frog couldn't hop out of. Eventually, her eyes lit upon grandmother's blue water jug. It was sitting where she always left it, on a wide indigo tile under the great cooling leaves of the tropical gem plant growing on her back porch. Emptying all but a little of the water out onto the roots of the gem plant, Nemimati dropped Costi into it with a gentle splash. Next, she ran to the nearby potter's hut to look for a pot big enough to put some wet stones and small plants in that would make him feel at home. She knew what vessels she could use and which she could not because the potter had been teaching her the craft.

Meanwhile, tired and weary after bartering with the vendors, grandmother Atl decided to skip visiting with her friends and headed home early. During the steep climb to her house, she drew comfort from the thought of her blue water jug sitting in the cool shade of the gem plant. After finally closing the garden gate at the end of the trail behind her, to her horror, she noticed the jug sitting in the dirt beside its tile and the water pooled on the ground.

Grandmother Atl rolled her eyes and looked up at the heavens. "Ah, that thoughtless child," she groaned. "I might as well send her to live in the forest with the monkeys!"

After setting her heavy basket down beside the large cauldrons of dye on her work table, Grandmother Atl walked over to pick up her blue jug. She supposed it felt heavier than usual because she was tired, so she didn't bother to peer into the dark depths where Costi clung to its sides with his little suctioned toes. After rinsing it out, she filled the jug from a height to oxygenate and cool the water as was the custom of her people.

Meanwhile, enjoying the unexpected shower, Costi floated like a lily pad on the surface of the rising water until he could peer over the rim of the jug with his little googly eyes. Looking for a safe place

to hide, after Grandmother Atl shrieked, frightened Costi dove straight into the cauldron of blue liquid. Blinded by the inky solution, he jumped out again, only to land in the cauldron of crimson dye. This time he climbed out cautiously and rested on the edge, slowly blinking his eyes and blowing brilliant rainbow and red bubbles.

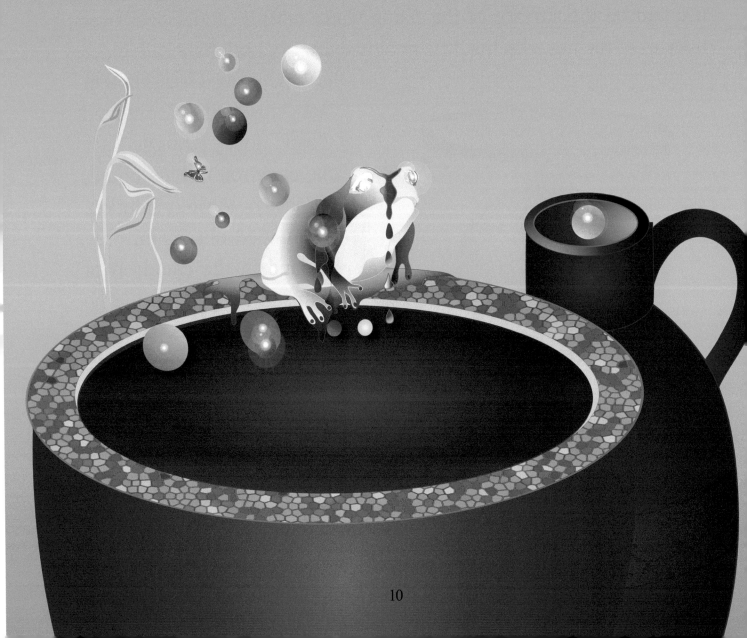

3 The Godess's Messenger

Exhausted Grandmother Atl collapsed into a chair and called for her granddaughter. "Nemimati, Nemimati! Where are you, child? Come quickly!"

Nemimati arrived back from the potter's shed in time to see Costi leaving curious tracks across a swatch of light blue cloth her grandmother had bartered for earlier in the day. After putting the frog away in the container from the potter's shed, she took two earthenware mugs down from a shelf. After filling one with water from the urn, she cooled and refreshed it by pouring it from one to the other before handing one to her grandmother.

Afraid her grandmother would soon erupt with angry words like lava from one of the nearby volcanoes, Itza and Popo, Nemimati stood by in silence. While still picturing the fiery volcanoes in her mind, she was very relieved when worn out Grandmother Atl only blew up a puff of smoke.

Shaking her finger at her granddaughter, she gasped out a warning. "The next time I catch you bringing wildlife into my home, young lady, I'm sending you into the forest to live with the monkeys!" Then she sighed and muttered, "It is becoming more than I can do to raise such an undisciplined child!"

Nemimati doubted that her grandmother really meant what she had said, because she had talked this way before. In any event, the golden frog leaving tracks on her light blue cloth had given Grandmother Atl an idea!

4 The Godess's Omen

Believing that Tonantzin sometimes sent messages by way of animals, Grandmother Atl clasped her hands in joy and looked up toward the sky. "Thank you, Tonantzin! Your sunny messenger, Nemimati's little dyed frog, just inspired me with a winning design for our tapestry!" She turned to Nemimati. "I shall show the goddess sitting on a cloud grasping the colorful threads of fortune in her hand. A life-giving sun, the true shade of your frog, shall shine down upon her shoulders! Around the border, I will space the seven forms of life, humans, animals, birds, fish, reptiles, insects and plants!

"Go see if Mishtla, the potter's son, has returned home. I will need some of the mysterious red Coloring Beans with yellow centers. If anyone knows where they can be found, it is he!"

"Alright, Grandmother," Nemimati replied cheerfully. "But what is so special about the Coloring Beans?"

"Hush child! It is said that their dye glows in the dark, as though by magic!" Grandmother Atl replied mysteriously.

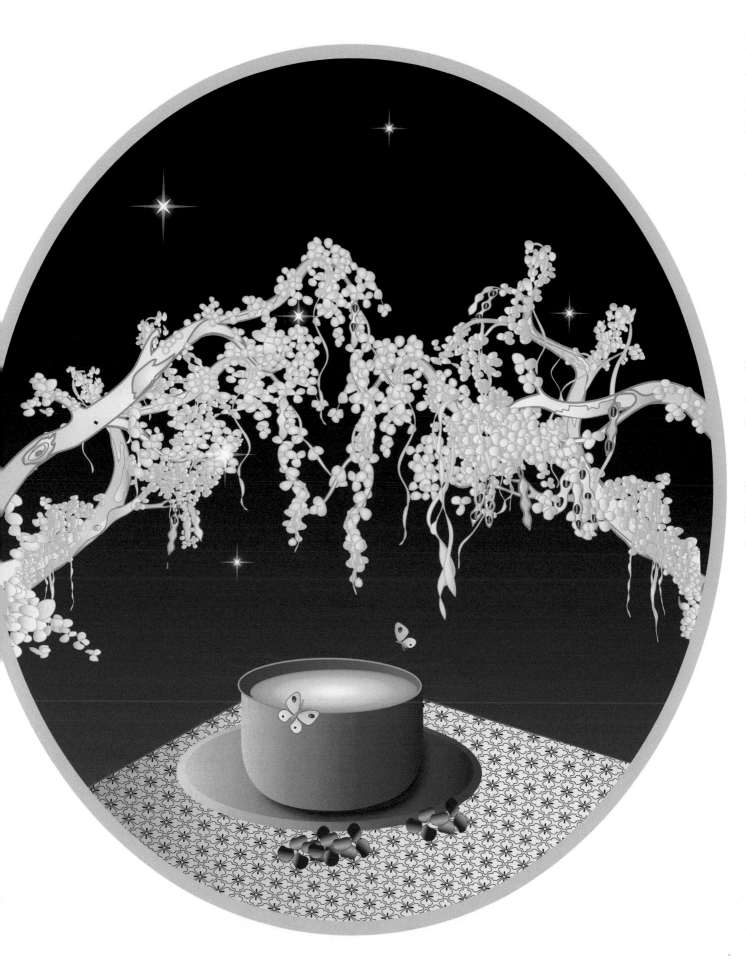

5 Mishtla

Nemimati found Mishtla, the potter's son, sitting beside a boulder sorting feathers into shapes and colors near his father's house. He greeted her with a big smile. "Hello, Nemimati!" he said. "Come over and admire my colorful feather collection!"

"Hello, Mishtla," she cooed, playfully taking Costi, the multi-colored frog, out of her waist wrap. Mishtla took a step backward when he saw it. "That looks like one of the colorful creatures that get washed out of the inky black limestone caverns after a storm! My father says the god of animals, caves and mountains, Tepeyollotl, painted these cave-dwellers of perpetual night with phosphorescent colors so they could identify each other in the dark!"

Nemimati giggled shyly. "Actually, this is just a little golden tree frog that jumped in and out of my grandmother's dye pots while looking for somewhere safe to hide!"

After chuckling, Mishtla listened as Nemimati went on. "You know so much about the wilderness. My grandmother wanted me to ask you to help us find some Coloring Beans."

Mishtla shook his head doubtfully. "That won't be easy. The season for Coloring Beans is nearly over and the unusually heavy rains caused many of them to mildew."

"Yes, I know, but when my frog left prints on one of my grandmother's fabrics, she got an idea for a design for the princess' tapestry contest. It's important, Mishtla!" Nemimati begged.

Mishtla nodded. "Alright. Accompany me tomorrow morning to the east side of the mountain to look for Coloring Trees, and we will see what we can find."

6 The Magical Beans

The next morning, Nemimati and Mishtla each picked up a big empty basket and walked along the path leading to the east side of their mountain. There they got a clear view of Popo, the great volcano, sometimes called *The Angry Mountain* because it threw up smoke and sparks."

As they walked beneath a gnarled tree growing amongst crumbling ruins, something sticking up out of the grass caught Mishtla's attention. "What is that?" Nemimati asked as Mishtla unearthed a golden coronet. Rising to his feet, he held the artifact reverently up to the light and then looked up at the tree.

"Look! I didn't notice before, but this is a Coloring Tree! Years ago, some adored queen elected by her people must have graced this garden in her leisure hours," he reflected. "This looks like the setting for a feathered head-dress! I'll carefully bury it back in the earth so her spirit remains at peace." After Mishtla finished burying the artifact in the earth, he looked up again at the bean tree. "Now we must pray to the queen," Mishtla whispered, "asking permission to gather her beans."

Nemimati raised her arms in a prayerful gesture. "Goddess of the bean tree, may we please have some of your beautiful red seeds with yellow centers so my grandmother can create golden dye?"

As though in answer, just then, a gust of wind caused the tree to shake its beans down into the children's baskets.

7 Gold Dye

A pleased Grandmother Atl gladly welcomed the children home. "Oh, thank you!" she exclaimed, "These Coloring Beans are the largest I have ever seen! We will soak them to remove the red skins and then after grinding the yellow centers into a moist meal, press out the dye."

After Grandmother Atl finished using her secret process to create golden dye, she tested it on a piece of white fabric that turned the color of pure gold.

When the village weavers turned out to admire Grandmother Atl's gold cloth, she explained about the Coloring Tree the children had found full of ripe beans. Since the weavers wanted to gather fresh beans for themselves, Mishtla and Nemimati escorted them to the ruins where the old tree had filled their baskets with Coloring Beans, but to their dismay, the ghostly tree had vanished.

8 The City of Tula

When a nobleman from Tula invited Grandmother Atl and her granddaughter to join him on his return trip to the Royal City, it appeared once again that Goddess Tonantzin had smoothed their way. Soon after their arrival, the two women visited a palace overseer

accepting submissions for Princess Itotia's weaving contest, at the Temple of the Morning Star.

"This one is exceptional," he exclaimed after unrolling and studying it. "Come back tomorrow," he continued, handing them a paper receipt made of bark pulp with hieroglyphs on it.

When Grandmother Atl and Nemimati returned the next morning, the overseer still had not arrived, so they climbed the temple steps to watch for him and admire the view. "What a splendid walkway!" Nemimati exclaimed, pointing. "It runs all the way through the middle of the city!"

That looks like the magnificent Causeway of Jade I have heard so much about," Grandmother Atl replied. "It leads from the steps of the Royal Palace all the way to the city suburbs." Next, sweeping her gaze to the base of the pyramid, she spotted a group of men dressed like the official they had met the day before, moving through the crowd. "Come Nemimati," she said, "let us go and see what those men want."

When Grandmother Atl and Nemimati reached the sidewalk, Grandmother Atl turned to a bystander. "Who are these men and what are they asking everyone?" she inquired.

"They are runners from the Royal Palace asking about a woman and

child from Cuanuac who submitted a tapestry to the Princess's contest," the man replied.

"That sounds like us!" Nemimati exclaimed, anxiously tugging on her grandmother's sleeve. "I hope our daring design didn't offend the princess. Her runners all look so serious!"

"Yes, I certainly hope no one took offense," Grandmother Atl replied anxiously while walking toward a man dressed like the overseer they had met. "My granddaughter and I are from Cuanuac," she said, offering him the receipt for her tapestry.

"Here they are!" the captain announced as the other runners formed up around them. Turning back to Grandmother Atl, he explained. "Princess Itotia sent us to find you. Come with us!"

The smell of fine perfumes and incense filled the air as the pair were escorted through a heavy wooden gate and along a walkway leading to a cottage. Although Nemimati had heard that Emperor Quetzalcoatl was reputed to be wise and charitable, when surrounded by the grandeur of the Royal Citadel, she began to feel small and vulnerable.

9 The Threads of Fortune

"Wait here until you are sent for," the captain instructed before ushering Grandmother Atl and Nemimati through the front door of the cottage. Adding to Grandmother Atl and Nemimati's confusion, servants soon arrived, bringing trays of food, fine clothes and fragrances.

"Be dressed by sundown," a tight-lipped matron directed. After the servants left, a warrior wearing an array of fine feathers remained stationed by the door as though on guard.

Nemimati helped her Grandmother dress in the finery they had been provided with, and then dressed herself. They then admired their reflections in a tall, highly polished mirror crafted from iron pyrite surrounded by representations of the fire-serpent, Xiuhcoatl, depicted with mosaic-work fashioned from turquoise.

Later that afternoon, Royal emissaries wearing green quetzal feather head-dresses came to escort Grandmother Atl and Nemimati inside the palace.

"The walls are so beautiful," Nemimati exclaimed as they passed glittering torch-lit frescos decorated with mosaics.

"The tile work is gorgeous, my dear," Grandmother Atl agreed.

As they approached the emperor's great bejeweled audience hall, they heard the festive sounds of many people celebrating. At the entrance, the first official they had met at the temple steps escorted

them through the crowd to a raised platform where Princess Itotia stood. Behind her on the torch-lit wall hung Grandmother Atl and Nemimati's tapestry, entitled The Threads of Fortune—its golden sun shining down upon Goddess Tonantzin as though lit from within by magical dye.

As soon as the princess had greeted Grandmother Atl and Nemimati, an attendant raised a ram's horn to his lips to quiet the crowd so she could address the assembly. "It is my great honor to present to you very gifted Grandmother Atl and her granddaughter, Nemimati," the princess anounced in her musical voice. "Their tapestry, The Threads of Fortune, has won my contest."

Tears of joy welled up in Grandmother Atl and Nemimati's eyes as the audience shouted with approval. At last they understood why the palace runners had come for them earlier in the day.

Grandmother Atl pulled a kerchief from her pocket and wiped Nemimati's face before wiping her own. "We are your Highness' humble servants," the winning weavers pledged after bowing to the princess.

Next, tall and majestic, Emperor Quetzalcoatl came forward, wearing his glorious Head-dress of the Sun. "How did the divine inspiration for this tapestry come to you?" he asked.

"It was like this," Grandmother Atl explained, describing how the golden frog, Costi, fortuitously marked her light blue fabric with inspirational designs. Also, she explained how, to color threads for her resplendent sun, she had wanted some of the out of season red beans with yellow centers. Grandmother Atl then suggested that Nemimati fill the emperor in on the appearance of the ghostly bean tree.

24

After hearing Nemimati's story, the Emperor smiled. "It sounds as though you were honored by a visitation from the legendary Coloring Tree."

"The *legendary* Coloring Tree?" Nemimati inquired curiously.

The emperor motioned to his steward, who then raised his hand to quiet the crowd. "Silence," he commanded.

10 The Magical Coloring Trees

"The story of the Coloring Trees is featured in the legend of Queen Huani the Weaver. When visiting her summer palace in the mountains, she spent hours under the boughs of her favorite shade tree, weaving at her backstrap loom. That was until a rival, envious of her weaving skill, concealed a deadly scorpion in one of her tapestries, leaving her fingers forever stilled among her threads.

"Upon Queen Huani's death, the priests proclaimed her a goddess and her shade tree a shrine. When after many years the old tree finally died, its spirit appeared and beckoned deserving weavers nearer with its gently waving branches. When they approached, it filled their baskets with perfectly ripe beans. Before long, the surprised weavers found that when dye from the beans was extracted a particular way, it glowed in the dark as though by magic. Although seedlings that took root in the wilderness grew up to be known as the Coloring Trees, their seeds never yielded the glowing pigment produced by the Spirit Tree."

Nemimati curtsied. "Do you think the spirit tree visited Mishtla and I?"

"There is no doubt in my mind," the emperor replied. "And your grandmother obviously knows the secret process for extracting golden dye from the beans."

Nemimati went on. "Hoping to meet your Majesty, my grandmother and I brought you a gift."

When Nemimati filled Emperor Quetzalcoatl's cupped palms with red Coloring Beans from a small woven bag, he lifted up his hands, exclaiming to the assembly: "Behold the magical beans with which Grandmother Atl created her radiant golden sun. I shall order them planted around the city, so that in years to come, all weavers may gather magical beans in Tula."

The spectators cheered His Majesty's proclamation.

After Governor Patli and Princess Itotia's wedding on the morning of the Spring Equinox, from a platform, Grandmother Atl and Nemimati watched the bride and bridegroom lead the Parade of Flowers. Beside the royal couple walked a standard-bearer displaying their tapestry, The Threads of Fortune.

The day after the wedding, Quetzalcoatl sent for Mishtla and his family, and Grandmother Atl became Royal Weaver. When Mishtla and his father arrived, they accepted positions as royal ceramicists, designing colourful ceramics for the palace.

In the years that followed, Nemimati attended the Emperor's renowned institute of the Arts. There she learned symbolism, astrology and astronomy, and mastered the revered craft of weaving and design.

Then in the year One Reed, on the Calendar Day of the One Reed and Ritual Day of the snake, to celebrate this very special occasion, Nemimati created an astonishing tapestry depicting Quetzalcoatl in his traditional head-dress of resplendent Quetzal feathers, for which he proclaimed her the premier artisan of the empire.

Note: The *Aztec* or Mexica *calendar* is the *calendar* system that was used by the *Aztecs* as well as other Pre-Columbian peoples of central Mexico. The *calendar* consisted of a 365-day *calendar* cycle called xiuhpōhualli (year count) and a 260-day ritual cycle called tōnalpōhualli (day count).

Printed in the United States
By Bookmasters